The Book of BOO!

Adapted by Marge Kennedy
Based on the screenplay by Mitchell Kriegman
Photography by John E. Barrett

Disney PRESS
New York

Special thanks to Shadow Projects, Shadow Character Design, and Shadow Digital
Designed by Joe Borzetta

Based on the "Winnie the Pooh" works by A. A. Milne and E. H. Shepard
Printed in Singapore
First Edition
10 9 8 7 6 5 4 3 2 1
Library of Congress Card Number: 2001095755
ISBN 0-7868-3364-5
For more Disney Press fun, visit www.disneybooks.com
Visit www.PlayhouseDisney.com

Fun with **The Book of Boo!**

The Book of Boo! features playful rhymes that make learning to read fun! Your child can complete each rhyme on every other page by reading the most important word in this spooky story—"Boo!"

Here are some ways for your child to learn and have fun while reading **The Book of Boo!** with you!

Be on the lookout for "Boo!"

The word "Boo!" appears throughout the story, on every other page. Before reading the story through for the first time, turn the pages and help your child point out each illustrated "Boo." In later readings, your child may also want to identify every printed "Boo" in the rhymes.

Play a rhyming game.

Make a game by thinking of words in different categories that rhyme with "Boo." For example: clothing ("shoe"); colors ("blue"); food ("honeydew"); numbers ("two"); and others.

It was All Hallow's Eve. The wind started to howl.
Pooh and his friends were gathered 'round Owl.
Owl opened the big *Book of Boo!* on his lap
As the wind blew the shutters closed with a clap.

As you read this story, here's what you do:
Search high and low for the scary word, "Boo!"

Tigger was bouncing. Pooh shivered. Roo shook,
As Owl continued to read from his book.
"How scary!" they cried—except for one friend.
Eeyore groaned, "Hurry up. Get to the end."

If the story can't scare him, then it's up to you.
Please try, as loud as you can, to shout, "Boo!"

BOO!

"What's the big deal?" Eeyore said to the crowd.
"There's nothing to fear, for crying out loud!
It's all just a story, and stories are fun.
Please wake me up when it's over and done."

Can Eeyore get goose bumps, like me and like you?
What would happen right now, if you shouted, "Boo!"?

Story time ended. The friends had a plan
For a Halloween party. The work soon began.
Piglet brought apples to bob and to eat.
Kanga and Roo made a big, tasty treat.

Will they wear costumes? Will you know who is who?
Practice your scary voice now. Call out, "Boo!"

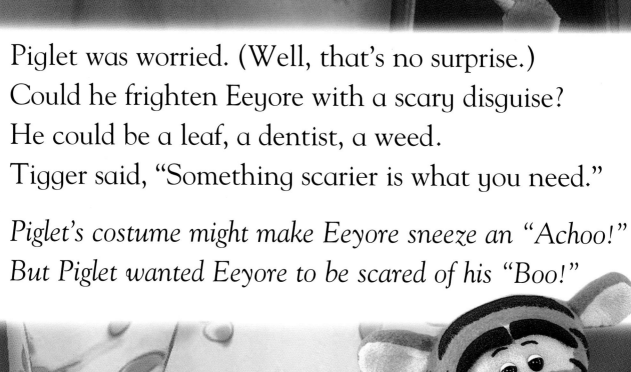

Piglet was worried. (Well, that's no surprise.)
Could he frighten Eeyore with a scary disguise?
He could be a leaf, a dentist, a weed.
Tigger said, "Something scarier is what you need."

Piglet's costume might make Eeyore sneeze an "Achoo!"
But Piglet wanted Eeyore to be scared of his "Boo!"

Meanwhile, Rabbit found Eeyore deep in despair
In the gloomiest part of the woods. "I declare!"
Said Rabbit, "The trouble with you is this place.
Pack up your troubles. And don't leave a trace."

Could it be that the gloom of his home made him blue?
Could that be why Eeyore had no fear of a "Boo!"?

Eeyore moved his house, stick by stick, one by one,
When three costumed friends dropped by just for fun.
Eeyore didn't even try not to frown
As Tigger, the wolf, huffed and blew his house down.

Eeyore wanted this Halloween day to be through.
He wanted some quiet. He didn't want "Boo!"

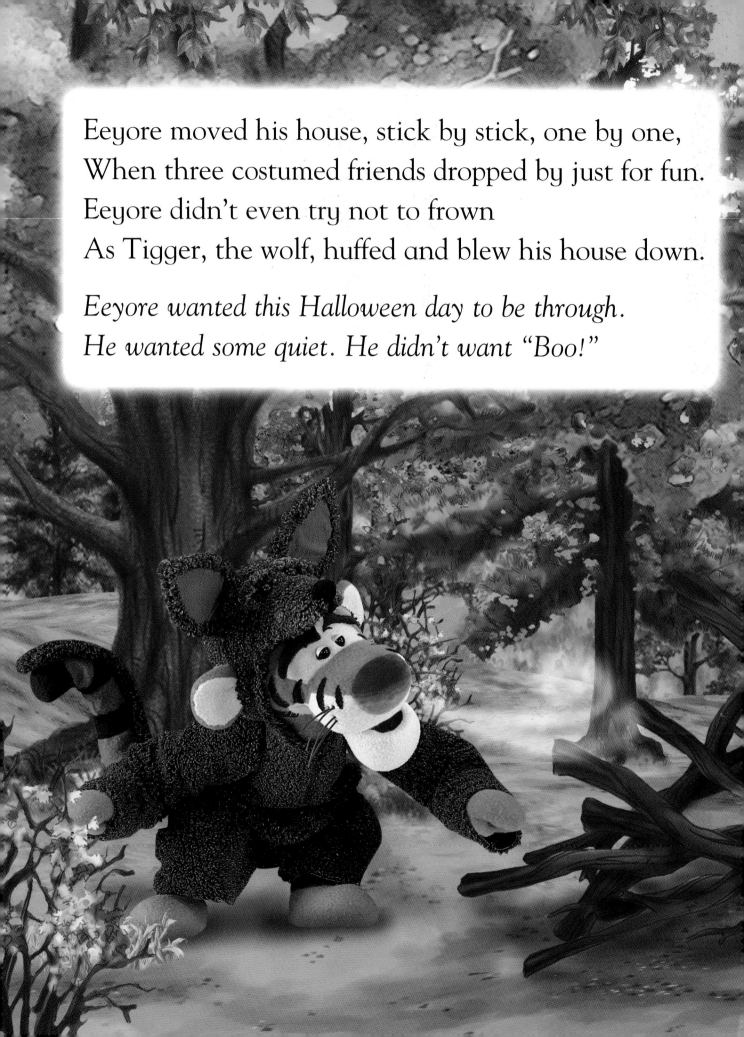

"I'm going away," Eeyore said with a sigh.
"I don't like this day. I won't even try.
No one will find me if I follow the sign.
In the deep Scary Woods, I know I'll be fine."

Eeyore just wanted some quiet, it's true,
Away from the hustle and bustle and "Boo!"

Back at Roo's house, the party was jumping.
Everyone danced. The music was thumping.
Piglet came dressed as a mountain with snow,
Saying, "Mountains are very scary, you know."

Someone is missing. Here's a big clue:
It's someone who's never afraid of a "Boo!"

The friends ran outside, shouting his name.
"EEYORE. OH EEYORE! This is no time for a game.
No hide-and-seek! It's Halloween night.
Please come to the party. Don't give us a fright!"

They ran through the woods as the wicked winds blew,
And no one dared whisper that scary word, "Boo!"

Asleep in the woods, Eeyore started to snore.
Till he heard the wind calling, "EEYORE! EEYORE!"
At that very moment, Piglet tumbled and fell.
He crashed into Eeyore, who started to yell.

Did Piglet scare Eeyore? Could it be true?
If that's what you think, it's time to say, "Boo!"

Yes! Piglet's arrival made Eeyore's heart pound!
He shook and he shivered as he lay on the ground.
But then he looked up and saw Pooh Riding Hood
And all of his friends in the deep Scary Wood.

Eeyore admitted, "I'm so glad that it's you!
I'll never again run away from a 'Boo!'"

The day was not over. It was time for the prize
For the scariest costume—the greatest disguise!
"I think that the one who scared Eeyore should win!"
Said Kanga as Piglet grinned his best grin.

The friends headed home, holding hands, two by two.
And together, out loud, they all shouted, "Boo!"

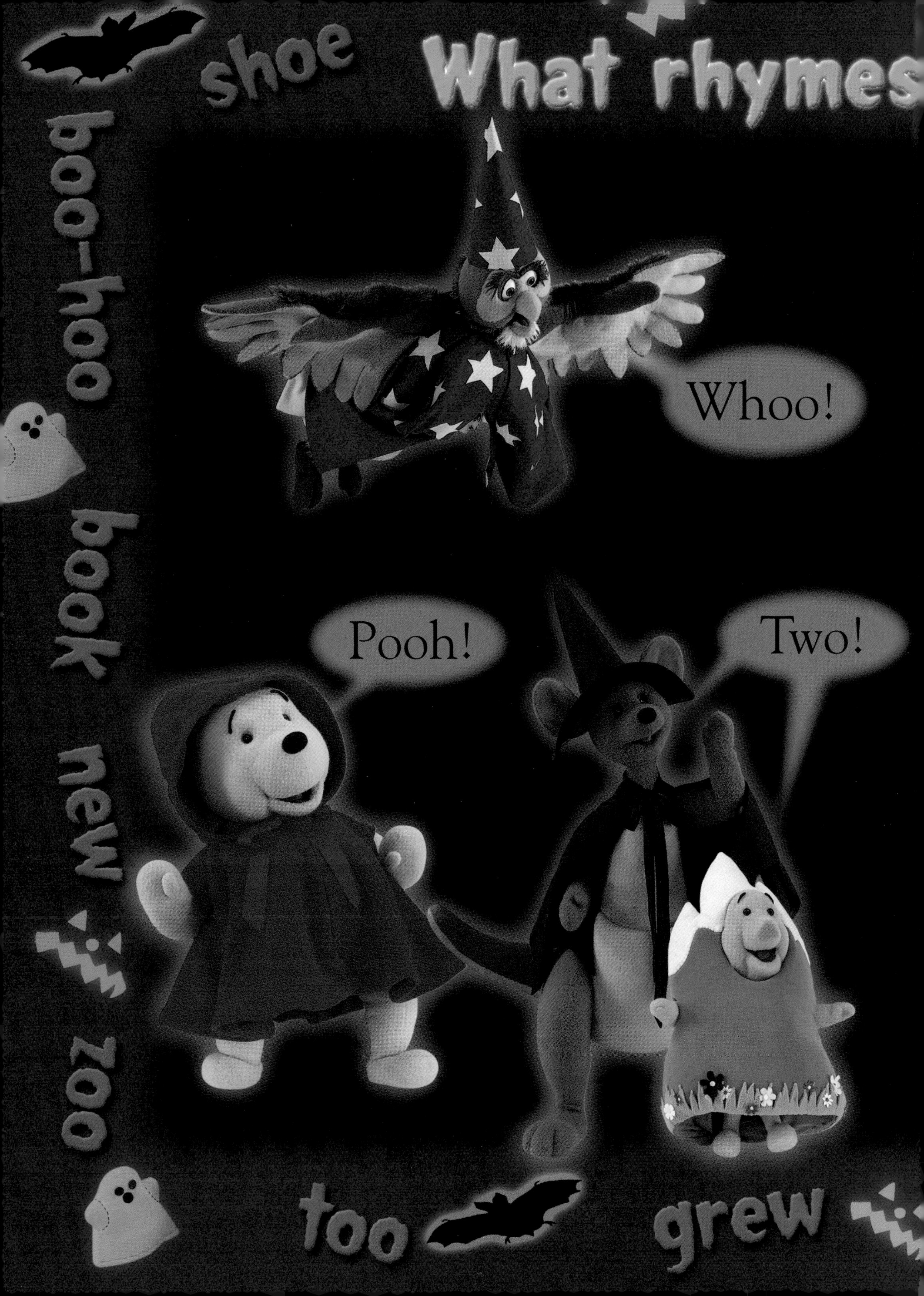
What rhymes
shoe
boo-hoo
book
new
zoo
Whoo!
Pooh!
Two!
too
grew

with Boo?

glue
kazoo
wolf
moo
goo
I flew!
Hoo!
Hoo! Hoo!
Boo!
I'm blue!
ice cream
donkey

More Fun with
The Book of Boo!

What other words begin like "boo"?

Encourage your child to think of other words that begin with B, such as *ball*, *bat*, *bicycle*, *banana*, and others. Your child might like to make *The Book of B* and include pictures of things that begin with the letter B. Your child can do the same with other letters of the alphabet, too.

Act out the story.

Once your child has had the opportunity to read the story with you a few times and knows the cue for saying, "Boo!" invite friends or family members to serve as an audience as you and your child give a dramatic reading of *The Book of Boo!*

Write and draw.

Offer your child a piece of paper and colored pencils or crayons and help him or her write the word "Boo." Suggest that your child add scary pictures to accompany the word.